Charlotte in Giverny

BY JOAN MACPHAIL KNIGHT

WATERCOLOR ILLUSTRATIONS BY MELISSA SWEET

chronicle books · san francisco

Dîner

(AUCUN PLAT N'EST SERVI POUR DEUX)

... — Pain de son beurré, la tranche, 0.40 — Beurre, 1. » — Citron, 1.75

...couvert, 3.75

Coquillages et Huîtres

...ennes la douz. 15. »
.... 20. »
.... 27. »
.... 36. »

...la pi...
......
. la do...
......
...né de Hollande, 14. »
...a cuiller, 20. »

- Bouqu...

...dwich au...

view from Appledore Island

Here's a picture of our ship.
It's from the breakfast menu.

April 24, 1892
On board the La Lorraine

I've never been on an ocean liner before. It was very exciting back at the dock. Crowds of people came to see us off and everybody waved and shouted. We waved until the crowds were tiny specks on the dock. Now all is very quiet and the deck is empty except for Papa and me. When I look over the ship's railing there is nothing but sea and sky. Papa says it will take the ship a whole week to get to France.

This journal was a going-away gift from my best friend, Lizzy Foster. I'll write down everything that happens, to share with her when I see her again. But that won't be for an entire year!

Our cabin is very small, with barely room to turn around. There are two bunks—Papa has the upper and Mama the lower. Opposite is a little horsehair sofa, where I sleep, and a tiny sink for washing up. When we want a real bath, we walk down a long corridor in our robes to a tub of steaming salt water. There's even a special salt-water soap for scrubbing! When the sea is calm, we can rinse with warm, fresh water. The bath steward places a pitcher of it on a rack above the tub. If it got rough, the pitcher could overturn. I hope it stays calm, or we'll all have itchy skin from the salt.

Wm M. Chas

April 30, 1892
Somewhere off the coast of France

Today it's calm again, and not a moment too soon. Terrible storms have kept Mama in the cabin with nothing but sweetened tea. Papa and I put on oilskins and made our way up on deck whenever we could. The waves were as high as a house! The sound of doors slamming and china breaking could be heard all over the ship. Luckily, the tables and chairs are fastened down, and the tablecloths were dampened to keep the plates and glasses from sliding.

A very important artist and teacher from New York is making the crossing with us. His name is Mr. William Merritt Chase. He even looks important, with his black top hat and long black cape! He and Papa spend a lot of time talking about "Impressionism," the new French way of painting. Mr. Chase says that Giverny is the perfect place to see it. Everybody paints out-doors, instead of in a studio, so they call it painting "en plein air," which means in the open air. I am going to learn more French words—as many as I can.

When we woke this morning there were gulls outside the porthole for the first time. A sure sign that land is near, says Papa. Tomorrow we should reach the French port of Le Havre. I can't wait!

Next stop...Paris!

Paris is *the* most exciting city in the world! Yesterday we visited *the* Eiffel Tower, an iron tower so tall it made me dizzy just to look up at it. The streets here are very, very wide and filled with carriages. Everywhere you look there are cafés. People sit at tables set out right on *the* sidewalk. Mama says that people here must have a lot of time on their hands.

This morning we walked along the River Seine with Mr. Chase to a store to buy art supplies. It's a busy river, filled with yachts and barges and tugboats. On *the* riverbank there was a beautiful lady with a parasol waiting for her dogs to be washed and groomed. And there were so many things to buy: not only books and maps but all sorts of birds, including a peacock. There was even a pet monkey for sale. He was wearing a red cap and a tiny belt!

After Papa found everything he needed, he surprised me with paintbrushes of my very own, made of squirrel hair. We said goodbye to Mr. Chase and went to *the* zoo at the Jardin des Plantes. I got to ride in a cart drawn by an ostrich. I'd never seen an ostrich up close before. I wanted to touch him but *the* man said I shouldn't get too close to his beak...or his feet! We had photographs taken—one to send to Lizzy and one for me.

The ostrich cart

MAGNÉSIE BL

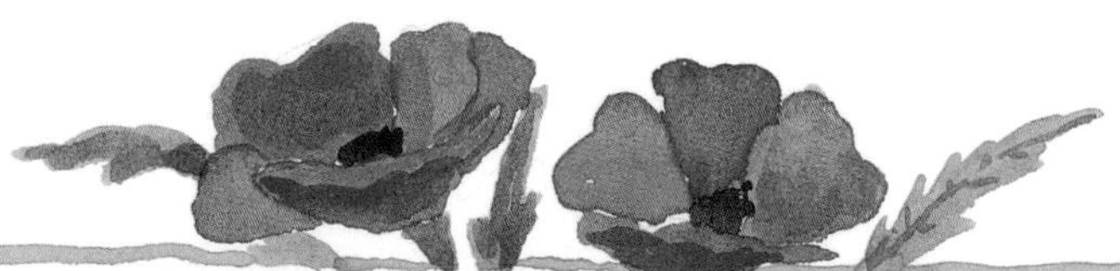

May 5, 1892
On the train to Giverny

The Gare Saint-Lazare is the busiest train station I have ever seen! A huge, noisy place filled with steam engines and tracks and smoke that rises right up to the big glass roof. Mr. Chase came to see us off, but as we waved to him from the train he disappeared in a cloud of white steam. All we could see was his black top hat!

We are now in the countryside and can still see the Seine. The train runs right along the river's edge. When I paint, I'm going to paint fat cows and bright red poppies like those I see in the fields. There is even a plowhorse wearing a blue collar with fur trim. I'll paint that, too! And women washing clothes in a stream and a girl my age tending a flock of geese. I waved to her—I wonder if she saw me.

The train doesn't go all the way to Giverny, so we will get off at Vernon. Papa has arranged for someone to take us the rest of the way by carriage. Vernon isn't far from Paris, but the train makes many stops—it even stopped once where there was no station to take on three boys with a canoe.
I can't write any more—too bumpy.

May 9, 1892
On the road to Giverny

The train station at Vernon was not nearly as busy as the one in Paris. A nice man was there to meet us with a white horse and a carriage. His name is Mr. Theodore Robinson. When I asked him how such a little horse could pull all of us and our luggage, too, he said the horse was small but sturdy. He also said the horse could rest from time to time because he planned to stop and take photographs along the way. "Studies," he said, "to make paintings from later." First, we stopped at a bridge where he took pictures of a countrywoman and her cow. Now he is setting up his camera where there are women drawing water from a well. He wears a béret and when I saw him I thought he was French, but he's not—he's from Vermont. He was one of the first Americans to come here to paint, so he knows all about Giverny. He says the smell in the air is wild mint. I've never smelled anything like it before.

May 12, 1892
The Baudy Hotel, Giverny

The hotel is a lot of fun. It's filled with painters—some, like ourselves, waiting for a house to be ready. Others are just visiting for a short while. Tonight at dinner there were twenty-seven of us, all at one long table. No one seems to mind a bit that people come to the dining room with paint in their beards! (And on their shoes!) It's very noisy—everybody talks at once and laughs so loudly that the dishes rattle. The dining room is filled with paintings, some painted right on the walls! Mr. Robinson says that when a painter can't pay his hotel bill he leaves a painting instead. He must know what he's talking about—many of the paintings are signed "Th. Robinson." After dinner everybody dances. I hear laughter and music long after I have gone upstairs to our room. Tonight I am in bed early so I can get up at dawn tomorrow. Papa will finish working on the house and I want to keep him company.

May 13, 1892
The Baudy Hotel, Giverny

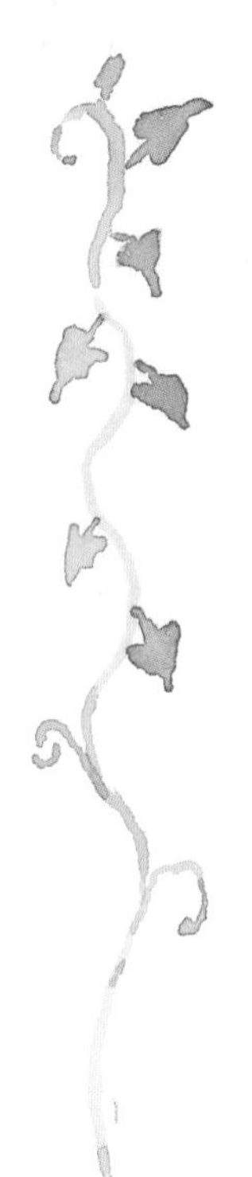

I love our little stone house and can't wait until we move in. Papa says it won't be long now. There are red tiles on the roof and the front is covered with vines. You can't see my room from the street—it's at the back, on the second floor. Papa just finished painting it—sunflower yellow!

Behind the house are rows of fruit trees in bloom. The air smells so sweet! At the far end of the garden is a stone wall, covered with thick, green moss. Then, a meadow filled with flowers and, just beyond, the River Epte. Mama says that when summer comes we'll have our own boat and spend lots of time out on the water. All the artists here do.

I miss Lizzy so much! Yesterday I posted a letter to her. I can't wait to hear back from her.

May 20, 1892
Rue de l'Amiscourt, Giverny

We have new neighbors—the Perrys. From my window, I can see down into their garden. There are three girls and a funny little dog that likes to bark and dig. Papa says they're from Boston, too. Mrs. Perry is a painter and Mr. Perry, a writer. I wonder what the girls like to do.

This morning, Monsieur Seurel, the gardener, helped me plant my very own vegetable patch. Only, he calls it a "potager." We put in peas, leeks, carrots, potatoes and lettuce. And strawberry plants all around the edges. When my vegetables are ready to be picked, Raymonde will show me how to prepare them. Raymonde is our cook. Today she made a special dessert for me—"Charlotte aux abricots" (apricot Charlotte)—out of ladyfingers, apricot jam and vanilla custard. It was delicious!

There is always a lot to do here. I don't miss school one bit—except for Lizzy, of course. And Mama says I don't have to have a tutor until September. Au revoir! Goodbye!

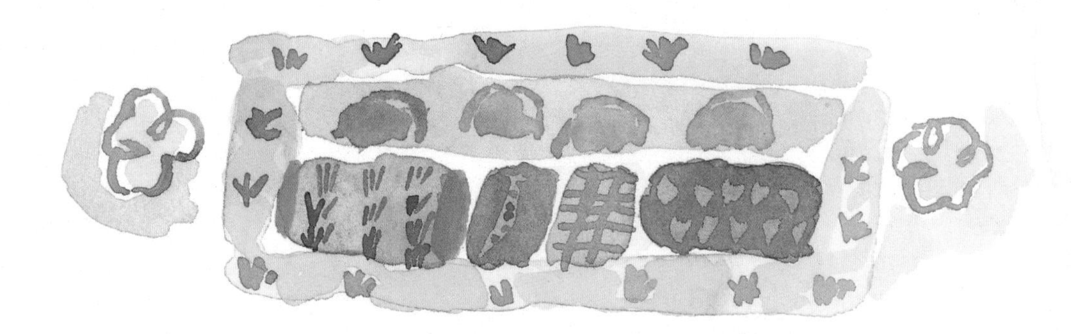

le chapeau

le ruban rouge

le petit chien, Degas

June 1, 1892
Rue de l'Amiscourt, Giverny

Today Mrs. Perry invited us to tea so I could meet her daughters. Edith is my age. Her sisters are named Margaret and Alice. Their dog is named Degas after a famous French painter. We tried to play ringtoss but Degas kept snatching the rings out of the air and running off with them. He's full of mischief and quick to learn tricks. Edith says he can pick the red ribbon from the rest of the colored ribbons on a hat and can bark "Yankee Doodle." I wish I had a dog just like him.

Edith spent last summer here, so she knows everyone. The big pink house on the other side of the Perrys' has a huge garden and belongs to a French painter named Monet. Edith says he is very famous and doesn't like strangers—especially Americans who might want to marry his daughters. He must like Mrs. Perry, though, because I often see them walking and talking in her garden. He has a black beard and a big belly and wears bright purple shirts.

Papa has started to build a studio at the back of the house. He says it's for rainy days when he can't paint outdoors. Also, for still lifes and portraits ...and for me, by invitation only!

June 2, 1892

A letter from Lizzy from Appledore Island! And photographs, too! It made me miss her all the more to see her picture. I wish I could be in two places at once. Especially when I read about all the fun they're having—fiddler-crab races and corn roasts on the beach! People here don't eat corn on the cob. Monsieur Seurel says that it's for pigs. And there aren't any blueberries either. Papa says he can't understand why Mr. Foster insists on painting in Maine when he could be in Giverny learning something new.

Lizzy

The Skimmer

la théière
Préparation :
un sachet par tasse
Temps d'infusion
conseillé : 3 à 5 mn
l'oiseau
l'arrosoir

June 6, 1892
Rue de l'Amiscourt, Giverny

Edith saw Monsieur Monet's daughter with an American painter this morning! Mademoiselle Suzanne was sitting by the bridge when Mr. Butler came riding up on his bicycle. When he saw her he jumped off, and they stood talking for the longest time. Just when Edith thought there might be nothing more to see, Mademoiselle Suzanne handed something to Mr. Butler. It could have been a letter, or even a book. Edith wasn't sure. Then he got back on his bicycle and rode away. What would Monsieur Monet say about this if he knew?

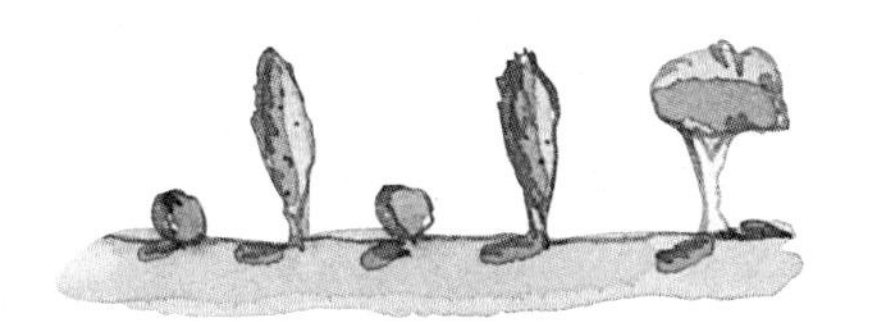

June 12, 1892
Rue de l'Amiscourt, Giverny

This morning we got up early and went down to the river to paint. Papa put his easel and paint supplies in the wheelbarrow. Mama and I carried the picnic basket and parasols. The meadow was wet with dew, but I didn't mind. I was wearing my "sabots," my new wooden shoes. Monsieur Seurel gave them to me to wear when I am gardening. When I first put them on they felt heavy, but now they're as comfortable as can be. I can even run in them!

When we got to the river, it was covered with mist. The water was as smooth as glass. Papa set up his easel and waited until the light was "just right." When it was, he began to paint very fast. When I asked him why he painted the same scene from dawn until dusk, he said, "It's not the scene that matters, it's the light. I'm painting my impressions of light and air and color." Mid-morning, when the sun came out, Papa showed me how the changing light made everything look different. By lunchtime, the meadow was filled with plein air painters and white parasols.

After lunch the sun was very hot, so Mama and I crossed the meadow to a shady wood. Just as we got there, who should we see but Mademoiselle Suzanne and Mr. Butler! They were laughing and talking and didn't see us. Mr. Butler was carrying his banjo and a picnic basket and she had a crown of wildflowers in her hair. Mama said it was none of our concern, but I can't wait to tell Edith. The Perrys have gone to Paris and won't be back until tomorrow.

June 13, 1892
Rue de l'Amiscourt, Giverny

When I heard Degas barking this afternoon, I knew the Perrys were home and ran straight there. Mrs. Perry was painting Edith's portrait. She had to sit still and we couldn't talk. I thought I would burst with the news! Then it seemed as if Mrs. Perry had read my mind. All at once, she surprised us both by announcing that Theodore Butler and Mademoiselle Suzanne are going to be married! And we are all invited! Mama is making a special trip to Paris to find fabric for our dresses. I cannot wait! I've never been to a wedding before!

The road to Edith's

July 6, 1892
Chez Madame Gautier
Vernon

Today we're at the dressmaker's having our final fittings. I had my fitting first. "C'est parfait!," said Madame Gautier, over and over again. That means it's perfect. And my dress is perfect—white eyelet with ruffles at the neck and wrists. Mama found everything we need for the wedding in Paris, from our hats down to our shoes and stockings. Even my hair ribbons, made of the palest blue silk. Now Mama is having her fitting and it seems to be taking forever. After we finish here, we're going to shop for things we can't find in Giverny, like special teas and cheeses. And for me, because I'm being so patient, some of those delicious candied oranges that Mrs. Perry often serves us.

Only fifteen days until the wedding!

L'azur
Le bleu
Le violet
L'indigo
le bouton
LOTION VÉGÉTALE
SUPÉRIEURE D'ORIENT
POUR LES SOINS
DE LA TOILETTE
ET DE
LA CHEVELURE
Le bouquet
Le Réveil de la Mariée
Vif, sans trop
Arrivée du cortège

July 10, 1892
In the studio, Giverny

Today is Lizzy's birthday. Bonne Anniversaire! Happy Birthday, Lizzy! I bet there's a clambake on the rocks and Mrs. Foster's gooey chocolate cake. And then a moonlight sail on the Skimmer. I hope my birthday card got to Appledore in time.

We have two boats: a large rowboat for fishing and painting trips and a small skiff for when we want to get someplace quickly. Sometimes, when we find something we want to paint, we stop and tie the boat to a tree trunk. Other times, we let ourselves drift with the current. This morning I caught a big shiny fish! But it was squiggly and slipped away, back into the water. Papa said I should try to catch another, for Raymonde to cook for supper. But just then the sky grew dark and we raced home from the river as a storm was breaking.

It's still pouring, but we're cozy and snug inside Papa's studio. I like the pitter-patter sound the rain makes on the skylight. Papa has been in a good mood lately and doesn't seem to mind at all that I'm here, as long as I'm quiet. It's probably because he sold seven paintings to a gallery when he was in Paris. Mama thinks he may have found a patron—someone to buy his paintings and help him become successful. I hope he writes Mr. Foster all about it. Then, why wouldn't the Fosters come?

Les poissons

July 21, 1892
Rue de l'Amiscourt, Giverny

The wedding was so much fun and even more beautiful than I thought it would be. Mademoiselle Suzanne looked like a fairy princess in her long veil and dress. And Mr. Butler was as handsome as could be in his silk top hat.

There were two ceremonies. The first one was at the "mairie," the town hall. The whole village came. I hardly recognized the farmers; they looked so different in their Sunday best! And Monsieur Monet's friend the painter Caillebotte sailed all the way from Paris—in a boat he made himself! As the bride and groom left the town hall, huntsmen fired their guns in salute. Then, everybody walked to the church for a second ceremony, where Monsieur Monet gave the bride away.

Afterward, we were all invited back to Monsieur Monet's "atelier," his studio, for a breakfast, which lasted most of the day. Then, just when we thought the party was ending, dinner was served in the garden! It was magical. Colorful Japanese lanterns twinkled in the trees. There was champagne (Edith and I had a sip—the bubbles tickled our noses) and iced grenadine with heaping plates of "crevettes"—delicious shrimp. I saw Monsieur Monet put so much pepper on his salad that it turned completely black—and it didn't even make him sneeze! Later that evening, the bride and groom left to catch the Paris train. Then, Monsieur Monet led us all on a walk around his garden which was filled with sweet-smelling flowers. I never knew there were flowers that bloom only at night. But Monsieur Monet has some! He also has lots of hens and ducks, including some beautiful little Mandarin ducks.

Just before dinner, when Edith and I were feeding the goldfish in the pond, we met a girl named Solange. Her father is one of Monsieur Monet's gardeners. Tomorrow, Edith and I are going to show her how to play ringtoss. It stays light so late now that it's hard to get to sleep. But I don't think I'll have any trouble tonight!

August 11, 1892

Rue de l'Amiscourt, Giverny

Now there are lots of vegetables to pick in my potager. I took a big basket down to the garden this morning and filled it up with leeks, peas, carrots and potatoes. "Bravo!," said Raymonde, and we made soup, only she calls it "potage." Mama said it was the finest she had ever tasted and that it must be because I tended to my garden so carefully.

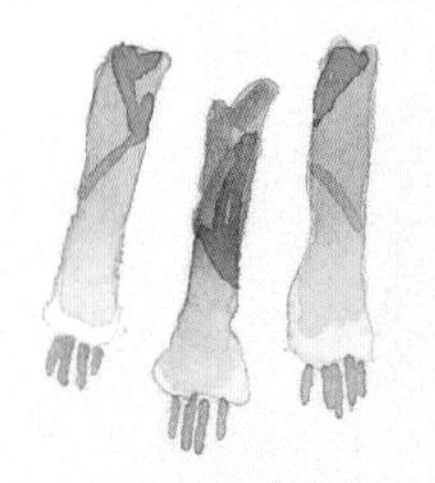

RECIPE FOR VEGETABLE SOUP

Wash the vegetables carefully—especially the leeks.

Peel and chop the vegetables (except for the peas!) and cook them in butter.

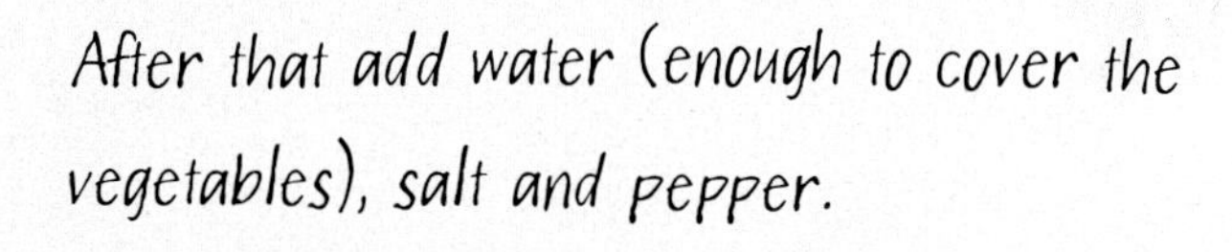

After that add water (enough to cover the vegetables), salt and pepper.

Let the soup cook gently until the potatoes and carrots are soft.

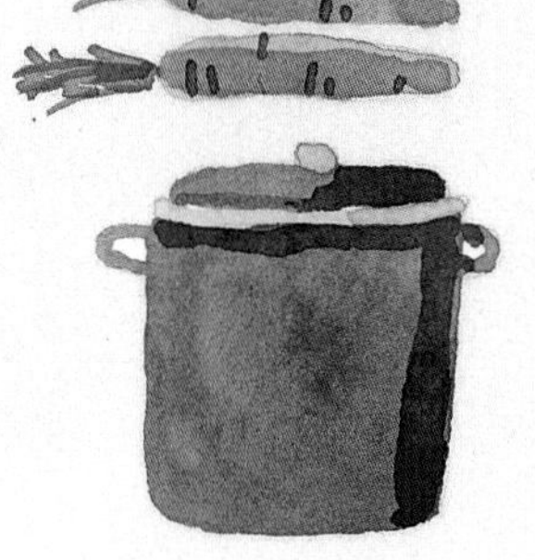

Voilà! Vegetable soup!

August 16, 1892
Rue de l'Amiscourt, Giverny

Yesterday, an English painter with a funny name (Mr. Dawson Dawson-Watson!) invited Papa to play tennis at the Baudy Hotel. They played against Mr. Perry and Margaret. Edith and I kept score. The Perrys won, four sets to three, so Papa and Mr. Dawson-Watson had to buy everyone a drink.

After the tennis match it was hot so we all went down to the river to swim. There was another swimming party already there. When we saw that it was Monsieur Monet and his children, we went on a little farther. Monsieur Monet likes his privacy. Still, I couldn't help but look back to watch him dive in. He made quite a splash! ⟶

While we were in the water we saw a very strange sight...Mrs. Perry's straw hat came to life! One minute it was on the blanket; the next, it seemed to be running through the meadow. We scrambled up the riverbank as the hat led us on a merry chase. Of course, it was Degas underneath the hat—up to mischief again. Everybody thought it was very funny—even Mrs. Perry!

August 21, 1892
Nettle Island

This morning, we drifted slowly down the Epte in the large rowboat. As we went, using short, feathery brushstrokes, Papa painted sunlight sparkling on the river water. Mama and I wrote letters. We have to sit still when we are in the boat so that it doesn't tip over. Edith said that last year one of the American painters fell in the river! He still had his palette in his hand. When he crawled up on the riverbank he was a sight, with paint all over his face and beard!

When we reached the Seine, we rowed the boat to Nettle Island and tied it to a tree. The island has a fine sandy beach for picnicking. While we were having lunch, Papa said if things continue to go well here he might like to stay on longer than a year. Mama doesn't seem to mind the idea. Of course, if Lizzy comes I won't mind either.

After our picnic we sat for a while, watching the river traffic. I never knew there were so many different kinds of boats. Steamboats and barges, sailing yachts and skiffs. We even saw the boat Mr. Dawson Dawson-Watson made for the new Mr. and Mrs. Butler. He made it out of wooden packing crates. Everybody laughed and said it wouldn't float, but it does—and very well, too, by the looks of it.

Then, Papa set up his easel. After moving Mama this way and that, he settled on a pose and began to paint. I was glad not to have to sit for the painting and went off to explore.

The cows at the River Epte

September 1, 1892
Rue de l'Amiscourt, Giverny

The other day, a man bicycled up to our house. His name is Mr. Philip Hale and he studied with Papa in Boston. Papa was so surprised to see him here! The Baudy Hotel was full, so Papa invited him to stay with us.

Yesterday, we went down to the river to watch the regattas. Mr. Hale said he wasn't interested in boat races and went off along the river to paint. At the start of the races, we all stood on the riverbank, waving our handkerchiefs to cheer the boats on. When the boats disappeared from our sight, we sat down to lunch at tables under the apple trees. There were stuffed eggs and little fruit tarts—as many as we could eat. Afterward, Edith and I took some cider to Mr. Hale. He seemed very grateful and I peeked at his canvas. It was of a woman washing clothes in the river.

Everyone else seems to be painting haystacks! Papa says it's because Monsieur Monet had such success with his exhibition of haystack paintings in Paris last May. One of the Americans, Mr. John Leslie Breck, was so inspired by Monsieur Monet that he made fifteen paintings, all of the same haystack! He painted it at different times of day, in different light, even setting his easel up in the middle of the night so he could paint it by moonlight.

JOHN LESLIE BRECK

September 4, 1892
Rue de l'Amiscourt, Giverny

We've been busy in the orchard, picking fruits as fast as we can. If we don't hurry, the birds get to them first and gobble them up! Solange and all three Perry girls are helping. We fill huge baskets with fuzzy peaches and apricots, juicy plums and sweet, black cherries. Raymonde is making jars and jars of jams, jellies and preserves—enough to fill all the shelves in the pantry as well as those in the cellar.

Today, Raymonde let us try her cherry jam. We spread it on thick slices of bread for "goûter"—our four o'clock snack. It was delicious!

September 15, 1892
Rue de l'Amiscourt, Giverny

This morning, the dreaded tutor came for the first time. When I opened the door she began speaking French and didn't stop until she left. I couldn't understand very much of what she said. I think she speaks English, but she pretends not to. Her name is Mademoiselle Bertout. Mama wants me to learn French and botany so we went out to the garden and I learned the French words for what I saw.

All at once, Degas appeared. He was covered with dirt and looked very pleased with himself. No wonder! He'd finished the tunnel he'd been digging beneath the wall that separates our garden from the Perrys. Mademoiselle Bertout tried to shoo him away with her hat, but Degas was much too quick and ran circles around her, barking as he went. And then I learned a French phrase I like very much: "La leçon est terminée." "The lesson is over."

When I returned Degas to Edith, he covered my face with kisses. I think he was saying goodbye. In two days they leave for Boston. Their trunks are packed and waiting in the hall and the house already feels empty. I'll miss them so much! I wonder if Degas will remember me. Mrs. Perry says he's sure to, because he's so smart.

le champignon
le gland
le papillon
la pomme de pin
la libellule
le radis
l'abeille
la feuille
les couleurs
d'automne

October 1, 1892
Rue de l'Amiscourt, Giverny

It gets dark early now. When I look out my window the garden is bare. Solange and I picked the last of the vegetables and put my potager to bed until spring. She showed me how to cover my strawberry plants with straw to protect their roots from the winter cold. Is that why we call them "strawberries?" I wonder....

I can see Papa through the large window in the studio, painting in the last light of the day. He is finishing a landscape he began last summer that is also a portrait of Mama and me. When I look at it I can almost feel the warm sun on Nettle Island and smell its sweet meadow flowers.

Tonight we are having mushroom omelettes for supper, "omelettes aux champignons." The mushrooms are from this morning's lesson with Mademoiselle Bertout, and Solange and I gathered the eggs from Monsieur Seurel's hens.

At first, I didn't want to go inside the henhouse. It's dark and smelly. Besides, the hens squawked fiercely and flapped their wings when they saw us. But Solange told me not to be afraid and showed me how to smooth their soft feathers. Then, ever so gently, we reached underneath the hens and pulled the warm eggs from their nests. Twelve big brown ones! Raymonde was happy to have the eggs and mushrooms. "Bien fait!," she said. Well done!

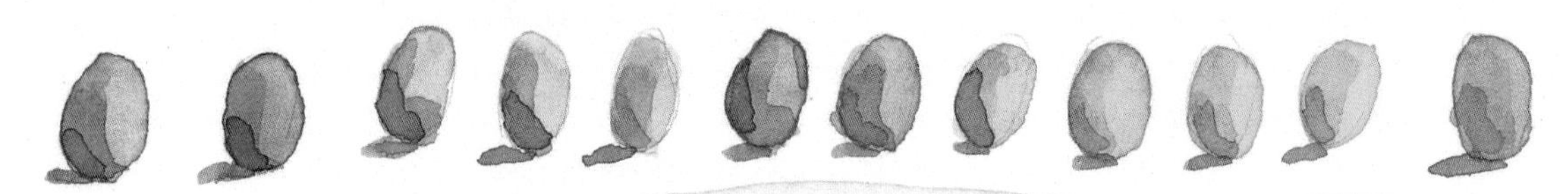

October 30, 1892
Rue de l'Amiscourt, Giverny

I didn't think we'd be able to have a jack o'lantern this year. I looked everywhere in the village for a pumpkin but couldn't find one. But then I drew one on Monsieur Seurel's market list. "Ah! Une citrouille!," he said, and the next time he came back from Vernon there was a big fat pumpkin on the wagon seat next to him. The French may not have Halloween but they do eat pumpkin soup! Papa says that if we're still here next year, we'll grow our own.

Solange came over and I showed her how to cut around the stem at the top and scoop out the seeds. Then we carved a face—the scariest face ever—and put a candle in. At nightfall, we put it on the garden wall and lit the candle. People stare and don't know what to make of it! Tonight, Papa and I went for a walk and saw another jack o'lantern glowing in the dark on a fence post in front of Solange's house.

The French don't have Thanksgiving either, but we will. All the Americans in town are going over to the Baudy Hotel for a big feast. Mama says that we'll have all the same things to eat that we have at home, except for cranberry sauce, since cranberries don't grow in France. But I don't mind because I don't like cranberry sauce anyway.

October 5, 1892
12 Acorn Street
Boston

Dear Charlotte:

Your father's letter made my parents green with envy. They talk about Giverny as if it's the only place in the world to paint. "An artist's paradise!," says Father. "Seven paintings sold! Imagine!," says Mother. My fingers are crossed.

Love, Lizzy

November 6, 1892

This came today. Can it be? Will it be? Lizzy ici ? Here in Giverny?

le bonhomme de neige

November 15, 1892
Rue de l'Amiscourt, Giverny

It's been snowing all day. I could hardly wait for Mademoiselle Bertout to leave. The minute she did, I went out to the garden to make a snowman. With Monsieur Seurel's hat and Papa's scarf, he certainly is a well-dressed snowman. "Très chic!," said Raymonde, Very elegant! By the time I saw Papa this afternoon, he looked like a snowman, too. He had gone down to the woods to paint. There was an umbrella over the easel, but his coat and hat were white with snow. And he had icicles in his hair! It wasn't hard to find him—all I had to do was follow his footprints. He seemed happy to have the hot chocolate I brought him.

Last night there was a winter ice party. After dinner we bundled up and set out by moonlight across the frozen fields. The marsh looked like a fairyland. Lanterns glowed in the trees like big, frozen fruits. Everyone was there—even the Monets. We put on our skates and set out. It was very still and quiet, the only sound the swish of skates on ice.

December 24, 1892
Rue de l'Amiscourt, Giverny

I'm wide awake. Papa says Santa Claus won't come until everyone is fast asleep. But what about "Père Noël," as Santa is called here? Does he care if someone lies awake on Christmas Eve?

We went to the Baudy Hotel tonight for "réveillon," a special Christmas Eve dinner. After we sang carols, Madame served stuffed capons and lots of cakes, cookies and candies. I was much too excited to eat, although I did have some of her "bûche de Noël," a delicious Christmas cake in the shape of a log. It looked just like a log you'd see in the woods, only, the bark was chocolate, the mushrooms were meringue and the moss was ground-up pistachio nuts. I brought a slice home for Raymonde to have tomorrow. We've left shoes, rather than stockings, by the fireside for Père Noël to fill because that's what people do here. And next to the shoes, a tall glass of cider and a plate of Raymonde's almond cakes, with a little Christmas note for Père Noël.

The tree Monsieur Seurel got for us is as big and beautiful as any tree we've ever had. The whole house smells of pine. When we were putting the candles on we noticed a tiny bird's nest on one of the branches. Mama says that's good luck. At the very top is our angel with golden hair. I didn't know Mama had brought her. She looks right at home in Giverny—just like us! Joyeux Noël! Merry Christmas!

Christmas Night 1892
Giverny

In all my life, I have never had such a fine Christmas. When we went downstairs this morning there was a tiny puppy in my shoe! He climbed out as soon as he saw us and scampered across the floor to meet me. He looks just like Degas, with a bright little monkey face and soft red fur. Wait until Edith sees him! I've named him Toby Keeper. Now he is asleep on the floor next to me—in the bed I made for him, a basket lined with straw. I hope he likes his new home. I know I love him!

Under the tree, there was a beautiful dress for me—red velvet! And a fur muff, as well as sketchbooks of different sizes. And violet candies, combs for my hair and a sparkling brooch!

Just as we finished opening our presents, Solange came by for almond cakes and hot cider. She brought a little toy farm her father made for me out of wood. It looks like the farms here, with tiles on the farmhouse roof, a barn and stables. There's a farmer and his wife, too, as well as a cow, a goose, a horse, a chicken and a goat. I'll keep it forever. Solange loved her presents, too—a pink angora scarf with mittens to match, knit by Mama. And from me, a box of those candied oranges we like so much.

A New Year's card from Edith. On the back it says:

Bonne Année! Happy New Year!
From Edith in Boston to Charlotte in Giverny.
Hugs and kisses from Degas, too.
P.S. I miss you, Charlotte! I'll see you
in the spring. Until then,

Love Edith

January 1, 1893
Rue de l'Amiscourt, Giverny

We had sleigh races last night to celebrate New Year's. Everyone came out to cheer us on. Even the horses were excited! They tossed their heads, jingling their bells, and pawed the snowy ground. Mama said it was the full moon that made them so spirited. It was very cold. We pulled the fur blankets right up to our chins. All at once, the starting gun went off. Papa cracked the whip and away we sped over the marsh. The wind was chilly on our cheeks, but we were snug and warm. Afterward, Papa said we had lost by no more than a nose. I could tell he was pleased by the way he patted our horse.

This year, for the first time, Mama let me stay up to see the New Year in. The party was at the Baudy Hotel. Right after midnight I got very sleepy. All the music and laughter couldn't keep me awake. Papa brought in blankets from the sleigh and made a cozy fur bed for me on the floor. But this morning I woke up in my own bed with Toby licking my nose and the sounds of Raymonde in the kitchen. She's making French toast for breakfast, only in France it's not called French toast! It's called "pain perdu," which means lost bread. That's because it's made with stale bread, bread that would be tossed out or "lost." They don't have maple syrup here, so I have mine with Raymonde's peach preserves. This is going to be a fine New Year. I know it.

February 12, 1893
Rue de l'Amiscourt, Giverny

It's been raining very hard and I have new rubber boots, just like Papa's. They come all the way up to my knees. This morning I walked with Mama to the "boulangerie" to buy bread and I splashed through every puddle along the way. When we got to the store, we saw Suzanne Butler. She's as pretty as ever. Mama overheard her say she's expecting a baby in June. I can't wait to tell Edith!

The flood

February 27, 1893
Rue de l'Amiscourt, Giverny

Everybody's cross because of the rain. Especially Papa. He's tired of painting in the studio day after day. Mama's angry with Toby because he had an accident upstairs. (He doesn't like to go outside when it's cold and wet, and I don't blame him.) And Raymonde complains about "la pluie" every time she looks out the window and sees more rain. The road to Vernon is closed and she can't get to market.

March 1, 1893
Rue de l'Amiscourt, Giverny

It's still raining buckets. When Monsieur Seurel came by with the eggs this morning, he and Papa talked a long time about the river. The river water has risen so high it could overflow and flood the valley. As it is, the railroad tracks are under water, so there's no train and no way of going anywhere. At breakfast, Mama said, "Oh, what a few days in Paris could do for me now!" But, of course, she can't get there. Now Papa looks cross and worried.

The only good thing is that Mademoiselle Bertout can't come and I don't have to have my lessons. Instead, I paint in the studio (oil paints!). Papa cleared a small space for me and a place for Toby's basket. I'm painting the garden as it looked last spring, when we first got here—before I met Edith or had a potager or set foot on Nettle Island. On my palette I have rose, ultramarine, dark green, vermilion, Naples yellow and cobalt. These are the colors I remember. Of course, Toby and I have to keep very quiet in the studio so as not to annoy Papa. On days when he doesn't want to be disturbed at all he hangs a little sign on the studio door—"Ne pas déranger" (Do not disturb)—and I know not to go in.

March 21, 1893
Rue de l'Amiscourt, Giverny

Now that the rains have stopped, we are very busy. Papa is up at dawn and off to the river with his easel. He stays there all day, painting in any light the sun and clouds may bring. On one canvas, I saw a row of trees bending over the river and their reflection in the water below. This morning he set out with ten canvases in his wheelbarrow!

Raymonde is happy again because she can get to the market in Vernon. But sometimes the market comes to her! This morning, when I was in the kitchen, a man poked his head through the window. I was frightened at first, but Raymonde seemed to know him. She bought nearly all the herbs in his basket...right through the window!

Last night, Mama had the artist Mariquita Gill and her mother to dinner. They're from Boston, too, but we met them here. Raymonde made a delicious dinner. We had "soupe à l'ail" (garlic soup), then roast beef, and meringues for dessert. At dinner, Miss Gill talked a lot about a large flower garden she's making for herself. She plans to spend the summer painting rows of white lilies, poppies and hollyhocks. I'm going to plant poppies, too, and pumpkins—enough for Halloween and soup.

Solange and I are helping Monsieur Seurel get our garden ready. And Toby, with his digging, is just as busy as everyone else. Mostly he's good about staying away from the potager and Mama's rose beds. But he does like to dig along the wall between the Perrys' garden and ours. Just like Degas! I wonder what Edith is doing right now. And Lizzy!

April 14, 1893
Rue de l'Amiscourt, Giverny

I looked out my window this morning and there was Madame Seurel in the Perrys' orchard. She had hung carpets in the apple trees and was beating them with all her might. Her face was bright red! When I saw that the shutters were open, I realized the Perrys are coming back! Hurrah! I can't wait to see Edith and Degas. And for them to meet Toby! I wonder when they're coming. I'll ask Madame Seurel. Maybe she knows.

April 14, 1893
Later in the day

A letter from Lizzy. Surely, this is the most special day of my life!

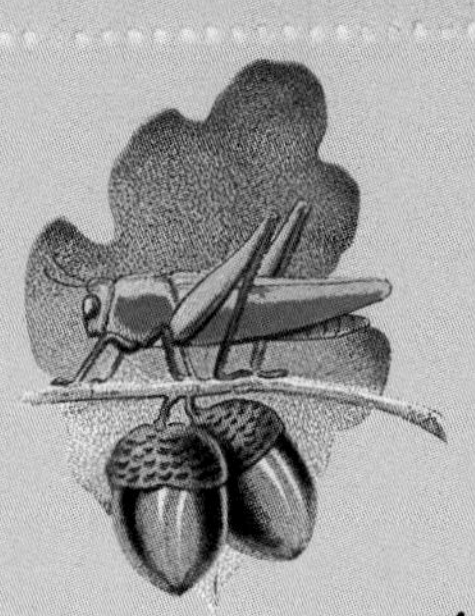

March 20, 1893
12 Acorn Street
Boston

Dear Charlotte:

Three cheers! Our fondest wish has come true. April 25th we will set sail for France on the La Touraine. We should arrive at Le Havre eight days later. I can't wait to see you!

Hastily and with love,
Lizzy

Madame Seurel says the Perrys will be here the day after tomorrow! There's so much to write about and I'm almost out of paper. It's three o'clock now...I know! I'll ride into town with Monsieur Seurel when he goes to pick up Mama. We can stop at the stationer's shop where I'll find another journal. While I'm at it, I'll get one for Lizzy, too, and surprise her with it. Then we can both write about the adventures we'll have together in Giverny.

I can't wait!

CREDITS

In order of journal entry

April 24, 1892

Photograph courtesy of John Maxtone-Graham of the New York Ocean Liner Museum.

April 30, 1892

William Merritt Chase (1849–1916)
Young Girl on an Ocean Steamer, c. 1884.
Pastel on paper, 29 x 24 inches.
Courtesy of the Warner Collection of Gulf States Paper Corporation, Tuscaloosa, Alabama.

May 3, 1892

Caisse Nationale des Monuments Historiques et des Sites
Children in the Jardin des Plantes, c. 1910.
© Seeberger Frères/Arch.
Phot./Caisse Nationale des Monuments Historiques et des Sites, Paris.

May 5, 1892

William Blair Bruce (1859–1906)
Landscape with Poppies, 1887.
Oil on canvas, 10 3/4 x 15 13/15 inches.
Art Gallery of Ontario, Toronto. Purchase with assistance from Wintario, 1977.

May 13, 1892

Mary Hubbard Foote (1872–1968)
View Through the Studio Window, Giverny, c.1899 to 1901.
Oil on canvas, 25 1/2 x 18 inches. Courtesy of John Pence Gallery, San Francisco.

May 20, 1892

Theodore Robinson (1852–1896)
Blossoms at Giverny, 1891 to 1893.
Oil on canvas, 21 5/8 x 20 1/8 inches.
Terra Foundation for the Arts, Daniel J. Terra Collection. Photograph courtesy of Terra Museum of American Art, Chicago.

June 1, 1892

Frederick Carl Frieseke (1874–1939)
Lilies, n.d.
Oil on canvas, 25 3/4 x 32 1/8 inches.
Daniel J. Terra Collection.
Photograph courtesy of Terra Museum of American Art, Chicago.

June 6, 1892

Theodore Robinson (1852–1896)
La Débâcle, 1892.
Oil on canvas, 18 x 22 inches.
Scripps College, Claremont, California. Gift of General and Mrs. Edward Clinton Young, 1946. Photograph by Susan Einstein.

June 13, 1892

Lilla Cabot Perry (1848–1933)
Child Sewing at a Window, n.d.
Oil on canvas mounted on Masonite, 21 3/4 x 18 1/4 inches.
Collection of Jane and Ira Carlin.
Courtesy of Ira Carlin.

Photograph © Collection of Monsieur Philippe Piguet.

July 10, 1892

Claude Monet (1840–1926)
Boat at Giverny, c. 1887.
Oil on canvas, 38 1/2 x 51 1/2 inches.
Musée d'Orsay, Paris. Giraudon/Art Resource, New York.

July 21, 1892

Theodore Robinson (1852–1896)
The Wedding March, 1892.
Oil on canvas, 22 5/16 x 26 1/2 inches.
Terra Foundation for the Arts, Daniel J. Terra Collection. Photograph courtesy of Terra Museum of American Art, Chicago.

John Singer Sargent (1856–1925)
Carnation, Lily, Lily, Rose. 1885 to 1886.
Oil on canvas, 68 1/2 x 60 1/2 inches.
Tate Gallery, London/Art Resource, New York.

August 16, 1892

Karl Anderson (1874–1956)
Tennis Court at the Hôtel Baudy, 1910.
Oil on canvas, 21 1/8 x 25 inches.
Terra Foundation for the Arts, Daniel J. Terra Collection. Photograph courtesy of Terra Museum of American Art, Chicago.

August 21, 1892

Photograph © Collection of Monsieur Philippe Piguet.

September 1, 1892

John Leslie Breck (1860–1899)
Studies of an Autumn Day, 1891.
Oil on canvas, 13 1/4 x 16 1/4 inches.
Terra Foundation for the Arts, Daniel J. Terra Collection, 1989.4.12. Photograph courtesy of Terra Museum of American Art, Chicago.

September 4, 1892

Theodore Robinson (1852–1896)
Gathering Plums, 1891.
Oil on canvas, 22 x 18 1/8 inches.
Georgia Museum of Art, The University of Georgia. Eva Underhill Holbrook Memorial Collection of American Art, Gift of Alfred H. Holbrook.

October 1, 1892

Robert Vonnoh (1858–1933)
Detail of *In Flander's Field—Where Soldiers Sleep and Poppies Grow,* originally *Coquelicots,* 1890.
Oil on canvas, 58 x 104 inches.
The Butler Institute of American Art, Youngstown, Ohio.

February 27, 1893

Photograph © Collection of Monsieur Philippe Piguet.

March 21, 1893

Willard Leroy Metcalf (1858–1925)
The River Epte, Giverny, 1887.
Oil on canvas, 12 1/4 x 15 7/8 inches.
Terra Foundation for the Arts, Daniel J. Terra Collection. Photograph courtesy of Terra Museum of American Art, Chicago.

All other photographs & ephemera collection of the author.

THE ARTISTS

KARL ANDERSON (1874-1956) Ohio-born Karl Anderson, brother of the playwright Sherwood Anderson, traveled to Giverny in 1910. Although Anderson did not stay long in Giverny, the figure paintings he did there are important Impressionist works, filled with luminous color, bright sunlight and shadows. In New York he was part of a group of six painters New York critics referred to as "the Giverny Group."

JOHN LESLIE BRECK (1860-1899) The son of a merchant-marine captain, Breck was born at sea and grew up in Newtown, Massachusetts. He visited Giverny in 1887 and became one of the original colonists there. He developed a close relationship with Monet, painting with him in the countryside and in Monet's own garden, and was greatly influenced by the French master's work. But when Breck fell in love with Monet's daughter, Blanche, Monet would have none of it, and Breck left Giverny for good in 1890.

WILLIAM BLAIR BRUCE (1859-1906) A Canadian painter, Bruce was one of the first founders of the artists' colony at Giverny. In 1887, he, his good friend Theodore Robinson and four other companions rented a large furnished house in the village and went out to paint the local countryside. Both Bruce and Robinson painted panoramic landscapes with similar compositions and may well have painted together, setting their easels up side by side.

THEODORE EARL BUTLER (1861-1936) In 1888, Butler traveled to Giverny. At first a guest at the Baudy Hotel, the Ohio-born painter became a permanent resident of the village when he married Monet's daughter, Suzanne Hoschedé. After the wedding, Butler turned to his home, garden and his growing family for inspiration. His pictures of Suzanne and their children, painted both indoors and out, reflect a happy domesticity.

GUSTAVE CAILLEBOTTE (1849-1894) Like his friend Monet, Caillebotte loved painting, gardening and boating. A frequent visitor to the Maison du Pressoir, Caillebotte would travel along the Seine from Paris on his yacht, often arriving unannounced. Monet urged him to lighten his palette and taught him how to paint the play of light on water. A wealthy man due to an inheritance, Caillebotte became an important collector and supporter of his fellow Impressionist painters.

WILLIAM MERRITT CHASE (1849-1916) Chase was one of the first Americans to practice *plein air* painting, although he was never part of the artists' colony in Giverny. Born and raised in Indiana, he was a brilliant art teacher and one of the most successful artists of his day. After studying in Europe he returned to New York to teach and, in 1891, established the first formal outdoor art school in the United States at Shinnecock Hills, Long Island. Often, he used his beautiful family as models in his paintings. *Young Girl on an Ocean Steamer,* may well be a portrait of one of his daughters, painted on a family summer trip abroad.

DAWSON DAWSON-WATSON (1864-1939) The first English painter to travel to Giverny, Dawson-Watson arrived there in May 1888. He registered at the Baudy Hotel for a two-week visit but, enchanted with the village, stayed for five years. During that time, he created a large body of work, many of the paintings images of peasant women.

MARY HUBBARD FOOTE (1872-1968) Born and raised in Connecticut, Foote received a travel grant which enabled her to go to Europe to paint. In Paris, and later in Giverny, she was a devoted student of the talented sculptor and painter Frederick MacMonnies. When she returned to New York, she became a portraitist, but while in Giverny her subject was often the village's colorful gardens.

FREDERICK CARL FRIESEKE (1874-1939) Originally from Michigan, Frieseke first visited Giverny in 1900 and settled there in 1906 with Sadie, his new bride. They rented a small cottage with a beautiful sunlit garden filled with flowers and surrounded by high walls. It was here, on golden afternoons, that Frieseke created many of the color-saturated figure paintings for which he is famous.

MARIQUITA GILL (1865-1916) Gill was attracted to the Impressionist style of painting after seeing exhibitions of the work of Monet and Camille Pissarro. She traveled to Giverny in 1889 with her mother and registered at the Baudy Hotel for the first of several visits. Eventually, they rented a house with a garden and settled in. At first, Gill found motifs for her paintings out in the countryside, but once her flower garden was planted she turned there for inspiration. It was in her picturesque walled garden that Theodore Robinson painted many of his figure paintings, including perhaps, *Gathering Plums.*

PHILIP LESLIE HALE (1865-1931) Philip Leslie Hale, a portrait and landscape painter from Boston, was a student of William Merritt Chase. He traveled to Paris in 1887 and lived there until 1892, spending his summers in Giverny. At the Hoschedé-Butler wedding, Hale was a witness for the civil service. In late 1892, Hale returned to Boston where he was involved with the Impressionist movement not only as a painter but also as an art teacher, writer and critic for the *Boston Herald.*

WILLARD LEROY METCALF (1858-1925) Metcalf, a Bostonian, may have visited Giverny as early as 1885, two years before the artists' colony was founded. Enchanted with the landscape, he returned, reportedly lunched with Monet and spent the afternoon painting with Monet's daughter, Blanche, also an Impressionist painter. By 1887, Metcalf was living in the large house he shared with William Blair Bruce, Robinson and the other early colonists. Metcalf's hobby was collecting birds' eggs, a popular pastime of the period.

CLAUDE MONET (1840-1926) Oscar Claude Monet was born in Paris but moved to Le Havre with his family when he was five. Even as a schoolboy, he was gifted and was encouraged by his parents and teachers to study art. When he was about sixteen, he met Eugène Boudin who liked to paint outdoors and was influenced by his work. In 1859, he returned to Paris to study art at Académie Suisse. In 1862, he met Pierre Auguste Renoir and Alfred Sisley, and together they founded an independent group of artists. They organized their first group exhibition in 1874. Monet's painting, *Impression: Sunrise,* gave rise to the name "Impressionism" and defined the group's style. In 1883, after his first wife, Camille, died, Monet moved with Alice Hoschedé and her six children to Giverny. They settled into the Maison du Pressoir, or "Cider-Press House," where he lived—painting, gardening and landscaping— for the next forty-three years.

LILLA CABOT PERRY (1848-1933) Boston-born Lilla Cabot Perry spent ten summers in Giverny with her family, staying much of the time in a farmhouse with a garden adjoining that of Monet, her friend and mentor. Perry painted landscapes as well as figures, often children—her own as well as children from the village. She bought paintings directly from Monet's studio and promoted his work as well as that of American Impressionist painters.

THEODORE ROBINSON (1852-1896) Born in Irasburg, Vermont, Robinson was one of the first American painters to travel to Giverny and one of the few to befriend Monet. Although Robinson was never his pupil, Monet offered to critique his paintings, and the two worked closely together from 1888 to 1892. Robinson's *The Wedding March,* shows Monet escorting the bride, his daughter, Suzanne, followed by Butler, the groom, escorting Alice Hoschedé-Monet. It is testimony to the artist's close relationship with Monet and his family. Robinson kept extensive diaries throughout his travels. These entries formed much of the inspiration for this book.

JOHN SINGER SARGENT (1856-1925) Born in Florence to American parents, Sargent grew up abroad and learned to draw and paint at an early age. A friend of Monet's, he was the most famous American artist to visit Giverny. Although he never stayed very long, Sargent traveled to Giverny regularly to paint outdoors with Monet and visit with his family. The two artists exhibited together in Paris and collected each other's work. Sargent traveled extensively throughout his life, capturing in oil and watercolor the scenic places he visited and the friends and family who traveled with him.

ROBERT VONNOH (1858-1933) An important Boston artist and teacher, Robert Vonnoh traveled to France for the first time in 1880 to study in Paris. Later, on his honeymoon, he would return to France, this time to visit the artists' colony at Grez-sur-Loing, near the Forest of Fontainebleau. An extended stay in Grez resulted in a one-man exhibition in Boston, and in 1891 Vonnoh began teaching at the Pennsylvania Academy of Fine Arts. Among his students there were Robert Henri and Maxfield Parrish.

Author's Note

Charlotte Glidden is not a real person, although there could very well have been an American girl just like her living in Giverny in the early 1890s. Her journal is, however, based on historical fact. Many of the artists who migrated there at that time brought their families with them. They went to paint outdoors in the French Impressionist style—*en plein air*—in the beautiful Normandy countryside. Some came for brief stays at the Baudy Hotel; others, like the fictitious Glidden family of this book, settled more permanently in the picturesque village and built studios near the houses they rented or bought.

Visitors are still drawn to this beloved artist colony, to paint; to see Monet's house and gardens, which have been lovingly restored; and to visit the Musée Américain, a beautiful museum devoted to the works of the American Impressionists who painted in Giverny. Whereas the paintings at the Monet Museum are reproductions, all of the paintings in the superb collection of the Musée Américain are originals.

I am grateful to Monsieur Philippe Piguet for the use of photographs from his collection, as well as to Madame Marie-Christine Bosson of the Musée Américain Giverny and Mr. John Maxtone-Graham of the New York Ocean Liner Museum for their help and interest.

Joan M. Knight